Which Would You Rather Be?

By William Steig

Pictures by Harry Bliss

JOANNA COTLER BOOKS An Imprint of HarperCollins Publishers

To Lily—W.S.   To Kelly—H.B.

Which would you rather be?

A duck or a fox?   A flute or a tuba?

A shirt or pants?

Tall or short?

Candy or cake?

A cherry or a plum?

A moon or a sun?

Asleep or awake?